Niwechihaw

—

I Help

Caitlin Dale Nicholson
with Leona Morin-Neilson

Groundwood Books
House of Anansi Press
Toronto   Berkeley

Kôhkom kesimamanew.   Kôhkom gets ready.

Nikesimanan.   I get ready.

Kôhkom otâpihew.   Kôhkom drives.

Niotâpihon.   I drive.

Kôhkom pimohtew.   Kôhkom walks.

Nipimohtan.   I walk.

Kôhkom âyamihâw.   Kôhkom prays.

Niayâmihan.   I pray.

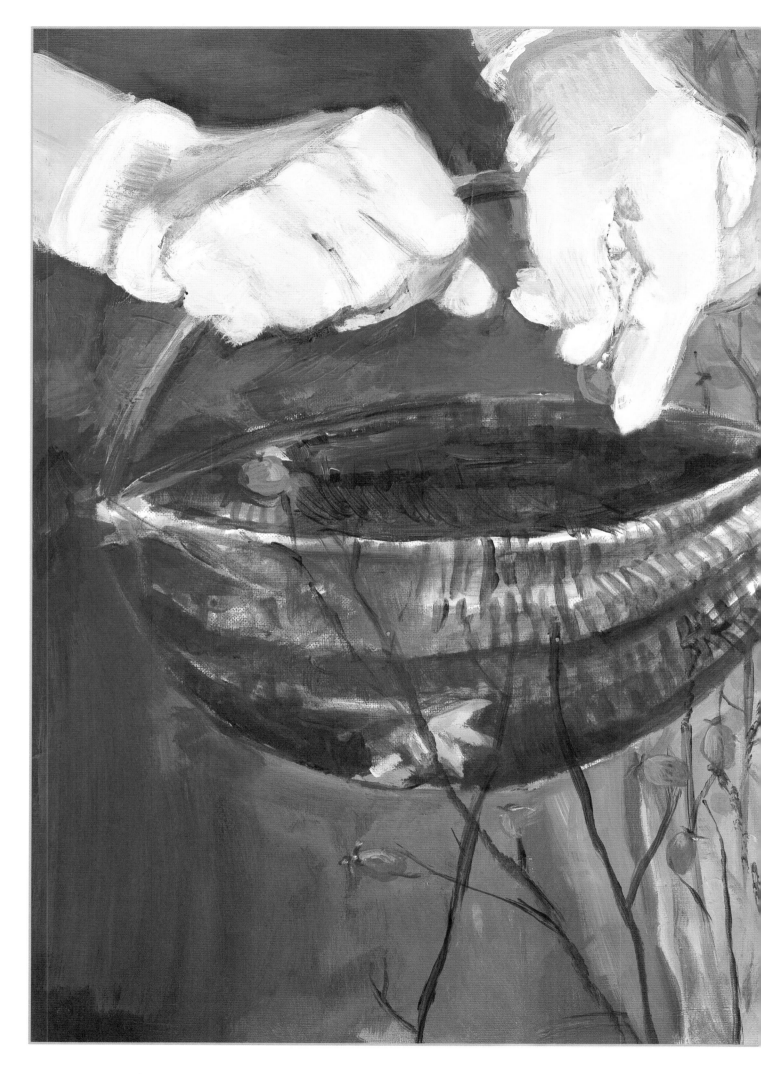

Kôhkom môsâhkenum.   Kôhkom picks.

Nimosâhkenen.   I pick.

Kôhkom nitootum.   Kôhkom listens.

Ninitohten.   I listen.

Kôhkom wechitaw.   Kôhkom helps.

Niwechihaw.   I help.

Kôhkom kisihtaw.   Kôhkom is done.

Nista nikisihtan.   I am done.

Kôhkom mîchisow.   Kôhkom eats.

Nimîchison.   I eat.

Kôhkom apiw.   Kôhkom sits.

Namoya niya!   Not me!

Okiniy Nihtiy

Nêwo minihkwâkana môskicowanipiy
Nêwo êmihkwâna okiniyak oskâyak ahpô pâstew

Akôhcimek okiniyak nipiyek peyak tipiskisow.
Pêtâ nipiy mîna okiniyak ta-pakâhtek.
Pakahcasis mitâtaht cipahikanisa.
Sekohkina mîna miyowâta!

Rosehip Tea

4 cups (1 L) spring water
1/4 cup (50 mL) rosehips, fresh or dried

Soak the rosehips in the water overnight.
Bring water and rosehips to a boil.
Simmer for 10 minutes.
Strain and enjoy!

Nicawâsimisak ohcî,
Garth Mâ Lê Nicholson (Dennis)
mîna Dalton John Nicholson-Tashoots,
kahkiyaw nisâkihitowin.
Nipakoseyim kâkike ta-maskawisîk mîna mamihtisik awina kiya ôma
Tahltan ayisiniwak ôma miyo mamitoneyihcikana mîna miteha. Ôma
masinahikan wapahtihew kiskinohamâkewin ohcî kihtehayawak ka
mekiskaw kiya. Moy wihkac nakî kiskinohamâkosiwin wiywâw ohcî.
Wiyawâw aniskomohcikewin kamiyaskamihk mîna nikanek.

Mîna sâkihitowinek ohi Shayna Dennis mîna Perry Shawana. — *Caitlin*

Nôsisimak ohcî
Austin Davis (Neilson) — Tipiskâwi-pisim,
Gabriel Evenden — Wâpos
mîna Avery Jade Evenden — Sîkwan Maskwa.
Pakoseyimowin kika-tahkonamin pikiskwewin mîna isipimâtisiwin
oteh nikan. — *Leona*

For my children,
Garth Mâ Lê Nicholson (Dennis)
and Dalton John Nicholson-Tashoots,
with all my love.
I hope you always stay strong and proud of who you are as Tahltan people
with good minds and hearts. This book reflects the education that the
elders are giving you. Never stop learning from them. They are the key
to our past and your future.

And in loving memory of Shayna Dennis and Perry Shawana. — *Caitlin*

For my grandchildren,
Austin Davis (Neilson) — Moon,
Gabriel Evenden — Rabbit
and Avery Jade Evenden — Spring Bear.
Hoping you carry the language and culture into the future. — *Leona*

NOTE

This book is written in Cree (the Y dialect) and English. *Kôhkom* is Cree for grandmother. In the Cree and Tahltan cultures, and in many other aboriginal nations, children have many kôhkoms. Young people use kôhkom as a term of love and respect for women elders.

MAMIHCITOTAMOWINA

Niwe naskweyasihmaw, nîkân mînamâwacinikan ôma nisohkamâtowin mîna iyinsowin awa Leona Morin-Neilson, Nihiyaw kôhkom mîna kihtehayah. Leona awasihkiskâkew ôma âcimowin. Niki misinahen oki pikiskwewina mîna niki sopihkahen masinipayiwina. Leona pimâtisiw ôma âcimowin kape kisikaw ohci awasisak ka – kiskinwahamawot. Leona wapahtahew maskawisewin peyakwan manâtecihwin, sâkihtowin mîna niwe naskweyasihtamek. Kiskinohamakew kayasohci isitwanihk kikawya anohc kîkway kespayik askiy.

Mîna niwe naskwe yasihtamek

Kehte-ayak Earl Henderson (Nehiyaw), David Rattray (Tahltan) mina Montgomery Palmantier (Tsilhqot'in / Secwepemc), ohcî Kiskitamawin ôma isipimâtisiwin, awasisak mîna kiskinoham-âkewin; onikihi komâwak mîna otatoskewak ohi "Power of Friendship" Aboriginal HeadStart program, Prince George, British Columbia; ni-kihci-kiskinwahamâto kesikiskinamakan: Nekanew – Perry Shawana, Dee Horne mîna Paul Madak; mîna Richard Thompson, Lisa Prokopowich mîna Kim Stewart ohcî nihtaw sehcekewin. Kinanâskomitinawaw kakiyaw ôma ohcî sihimew mîna ni – sohkamâtowin.

ACKNOWLEDGMENTS

I'd like to acknowledge, first and foremost, the support and the wisdom of Leona Morin-Neilson, Cree grandmother and elder. Leona was the inspiration for this book. I wrote the words and painted the scenes. Leona created this story off the written page. She makes this story a reality each day through her interactions with children and the deep respect and commitment she shows to them. With her teaching and storytelling, she gives young people the tools they need to live with traditional values in a contemporary world.

I'd also like to acknowledge

Elders Earl Henderson (Cree), David Rattray (Tahltan) and Montgomery Palmantier (Tsilhqot'in / Secwepemc) for their knowledge of culture, children and education; parents, families and staff of the "Power of Friendship" Aboriginal HeadStart program in Prince George, British Columbia; my UNBC Graduate Committee – Supervisor Perry Shawana, Dee Horne and Paul Madak; and Richard Thompson, Lisa Prokopowich and Kim Stewart for their technical advice. Thank you all for your encouragement and support.

Groundwood Books / House of Anansi Press
110 Spadina Avenue, Suite 801
Toronto, Ontario M5V 2K4
Distributed in the USA by Publishers Group West
1700 Fourth Street, Berkeley, CA 94710

We acknowledge for their financial support of our publishing program the Canada Council for the Arts, the Government of Canada through the Book Publishing Industry Development Program (BPIDP) and the Ontario Arts Council.

 Canada Council   Conseil des Arts
for the Arts   du Canada

 ONTARIO ARTS COUNCIL
CONSEIL DES ARTS DE L'ONTARIO

Library and Archives Canada Cataloguing in Publication
Nicholson, Caitlin Dale
Niwechihaw = I help / Caitlin Dale Nicholson ; with Leona Morin-Neilson.
Text in Cree and English.
ISBN-13: 978-0-88899-812-5
ISBN-10: 0-88899-812-0
1. Cree Indians–Social life and customs–Juvenile fiction.
I. Morin-Neilson, Leona II. Title.
PS8627.I22N58 2007   jC897'.323   C2007-904824-2

The illustrations were done in acrylics.
Printed and bound in China